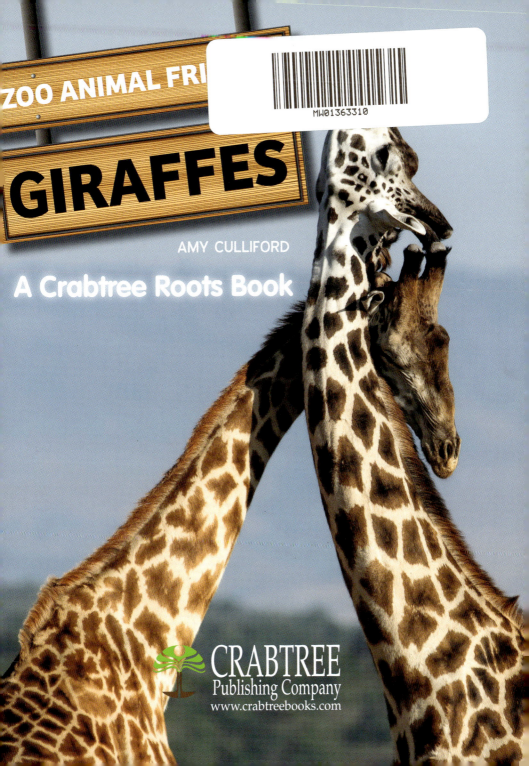

ZOO ANIMAL FRIENDS

GIRAFFES

AMY CULLIFORD

A Crabtree Roots Book

CRABTREE
Publishing Company
www.crabtreebooks.com

School-to-Home Support for Caregivers and Teachers

This book helps children grow by letting them practice reading. Here are a few guiding questions to help the reader with building his or her comprehension skills. Possible answers appear here in red.

Before Reading:
- What do I think this book is about?
  - *I think this book is about giraffes.*
  - *I think this book is about what giraffes like to do.*
- What do I want to learn about this topic?
  - *I want to learn what giraffes drink.*
  - *I want to learn what colors a giraffe can be.*

During Reading:
- I wonder why…
  - *I wonder why giraffes are tall.*
  - *I wonder why giraffes eat so much.*
- What have I learned so far?
  - *I have learned that giraffes can run.*
  - *I have learned that giraffes drink water.*

After Reading:
- What details did I learn about this topic?
  - *I have learned that giraffes have long necks.*
  - *I have learned that giraffes can be white, yellow, and brown.*
- Read the book again and look for the vocabulary words.
  - *I see the word **tall** on page 6 and the word **drink** on page 12. The other vocabulary word is found on page 14.*

This is a **giraffe**.

Most giraffes are white, yellow, and brown.

Most giraffes are **tall**.

All giraffes can run.

Most giraffes eat all day.

All giraffes **drink** water.

Word List

Sight Words

a	are	is
all	can	most
and	eat	this

Words to Know

drink giraffe tall

28 Words

This is a **giraffe**.

Most giraffes are white, yellow, and brown.

Most giraffes are **tall**.

All giraffes can run.

Most giraffes eat all day.

All giraffes **drink** water.

Written by: Amy Culliford
Designed by: Rhea Wallace
Series Development : James Earley
Proofreader: Janine Deschenes
Educational Consultant: Marie Lemke M.Ed.

Photographs:
Shutterstock: Gastan Piccinetti: cover; Chaithanya Krishan: p. 1; Bambi2020: p. 3, 14; RMFerreira: p. 5; Smithy55: p. 7, 14; Jeannette Katzier: p. 8; JOel Shawn: p. 11; Stacey Ann Alberts: p. 12-13, 14

Library and Archives Canada Cataloguing in Publication

Title: Giraffes / Amy Culliford.
Names: Culliford, Amy, 1992- author.
Description: Series statement: Zoo animal friends | "A Crabtree roots book".
Identifiers: Canadiana (print) 20210178337 |
  Canadiana (ebook) 20210178345 |
  ISBN 9781427160348 (hardcover) |
  ISBN 9781427160409 (softcover) |
  ISBN 9781427133250 (HTML) |
  ISBN 9781427133854 (EPUB) |
  ISBN 9781427160584 (read-along ebook)
Subjects: LCSH: Giraffe—Juvenile literature.
Classification: LCC QL795.G55 C85 2022 | DDC j599.638—dc23

Library of Congress Cataloging-in-Publication Data

Names: Culliford, Amy, 1992- author.
Title: Giraffes / Amy Culliford.
Description: New York : Crabtree Publishing, [2022] | Series: Zoo animal friends - a Crabtree roots book | Includes index. | Audience: Ages 4-6 | Audience: Grades K-1
Identifiers: LCCN 2021014543 (print) | LCCN 2021014544 (ebook) |
  ISBN 9781427160348 (hardcover) |
  ISBN 9781427160409 (paperback) |
  ISBN 9781427133250 (ebook) |
  ISBN 9781427133854 (epub) |
  ISBN 9781427160584
Subjects: LCSH: Giraffe--Juvenile literature. | Zoo animals--Juvenile literature.
Classification: LCC SF408.6.G57 C85 2022 (print) | LCC SF408.6.G57 (ebook) | DDC 599.638--dc23
LC record available at https://lccn.loc.gov/2021014543
LC ebook record available at https://lccn.loc.gov/2021014544

Crabtree Publishing Company

www.crabtreebooks.com   1-800-387-7650

Copyright © 2022 **CRABTREE PUBLISHING COMPANY**   Printed in the U.S.A./062021/CG20210401

All rights reserved. No part of this publication may be reproduced, stored in a retrieval system or be transmitted in any form or by any means, electronic, mechanical, photocopying, recording, or otherwise, without the prior written permission of Crabtree Publishing Company. In Canada: We acknowledge the financial support of the Government of Canada through the Canada Book Fund for our publishing activities.

Published in the United States
Crabtree Publishing
347 Fifth Avenue, Suite 1402-145
New York, NY, 10016

Published in Canada
Crabtree Publishing
616 Welland Ave.
St. Catharines, Ontario L2M 5V6